FLEDGLING

SONG

Hey neighbor —
I wrote this short story
longish!
a while ago + still
think it's pretty good.
Enjoy + pass it on!
Abbey

FLEDGLING

SONG

Abbey von Gohren

eLectio Publishing
Little Elm, TX
www.eLectioPublishing.com

Fledgling Song
Abbey von Gohen

Copyright © 2013 by Abbey von Gohren
Cover Copyright © 2013 by eLectio Publishing
Cover Photo by Abbey von Gohren

ISBN: 0615858678
ISBN-13: 978-0615858678

ACKNOWLEDGMENTS

I would like to thank Robbie and Henry Lewis for being my very first readers, for showing me how to recognize beauty in language, and for teaching me that a love of words is expressed by editors and poets alike. (Not to mention that this book may not have seen the light of day without you!)

To my husband, Karl, who reads me best of all. I love you.

Many thanks to Gabrielle Sedita and Elizabeth Brahy, for many café meetings and cross-Atlantic edits at the very beginning of this winding story.

Thank you to my dear Lisa Heaner for her careful—and enraptured—readings.

My sincere gratitude to the wonderful literary family that has adopted me at eLectio Publishing. Thanks to Jesse Greever and Christopher Dixon for reading my work, offering their encouragement and guidance, and sparking a relationship for hopefully many fruitful years to come.

To all my readers at   lifelongfling.blogspot.com: thank you for your faithful and exuberant following over the years.

Finally, *merci à Paris*. I couldn't have done it without you.

FLEDGLING SONG

This place is as sodden as the summer wetlands that I know. A grey haze lies low in the landscape, permeates the air, diffuses the sunlight into a pale imitation. Nearby, Canada geese honk out of impatience, and finally lay full on their horns in a chorus of protest. A few redwing blackbirds attempt to keep the peace, but their jeering whistles go ignored for the most part. If I listen carefully underneath the din, I can catch the ambient hum of the insects which rises and fades erratically like an old electric motor . . . .

***

Claire put down her pen and sighed. The sound of the dehumidifier was not really like that of the cicadas from her Manitoba home, but she had believed it—if only for a second. She leaned over from her perch on the radiator and eyed her present surroundings through the green metal shutters, cocked open just barely wide enough to focus on a narrow sample of the rue de l'Hopitâl. An otherwise calm morning was punctuated by drivers gustily airing their ire at a nearby intersection, while a bored police officer directed the impatient vehicles.

The drone of the machine in the corner was growing tiresome, but Claire had resolved to put up with it, mostly to please her neighbor. The gray man who lived one floor below had gone to the trouble of wrangling the ancient-looking contraption up the crooked flight of stairs that separated his door from hers, and she figured that her thanks echoed in the incessant rumble in the floorboards. Claire had felt a little knot of excitement form in her stomach when he had knocked. Her first visitor in four months. His close-knit eyebrows were usually focused inward and seemed to warn: do not disturb. But she often wondered about him, his solitary life. He could have been her grandfather. On Sundays, she would lay her head on the rough floor and strain her ear to listen whether anyone came to visit. So far, there had been nothing but silence.

Until that morning, that is, when he had materialized on her doorstep and opened his mouth to speak. His words seemed filtered through the mass of wiry, silver whiskers. He was gruff but friendly, and delivered the machine with a cheery warning,

"Make sure if it sputters, you stand back. The last time it shorted out, I got a devil of a shock." Claire smiled nervously and offered him a towel for his hands and face, already glistening with beads of moisture from standing in her doorway. She thanked him profusely.

"Er—monsieur," she almost said sir, falling into English, as his accent was unmistakably non-French. However, some odd sense of propriety kept her speaking a language foreign to the both of them. "When should I-"

"Don't worry about returning it until May. Beh, you'll need it." One knowing eye glinted from under the shelter of his black brow, and lifting his hat, he wished her a bonne journée. Closing the door on his broad, square back, Claire peered skeptically at the special delivery. She walked past it gingerly to a minuscule square of Formica in the corner and started the tea kettle, which, depressingly, raised the dew point even higher. After a long moment, she tentatively plugged it in, and picked up her notebook where she had left off.

**

The water forms in pools at the base of the windowsills. Sometimes I have to clear away the mold that begins to encroach around these ponds, and I imagine what the discolored water would look like under a microscope. Probably nothing terribly interesting — maybe some bacteria if I were lucky. Amoebae finding themselves worlds away from their place of origin, cramped in a tiny spot of water, instead of the broad woods and wilds. At least they're meant to be aquatic creatures. Ah, me. I long for an arid northern tundra. If only these droplets hanging about everything would cling to one another instead, and form a flurry of frozen beauties. Yes, precipitation would be infinitely more appreciable in the form of snow.

3

The only oasis of dry heat in her apartment was the radiator, which was almost painfully hot. She usually sat on it anyway, and a pleasant burn would seep into her bones. Spots on her jeans still damp from the washing would finally disappear. Normally, her laundry had to hang on a flimsy drying rack for days. It was one of her funny little ways of economizing that became a burden more than anything. *I'm a poor student; this is the way things are.* Claire sighed and looked at the T-shirts and underwear drooping under the weight of the wet room, just as soggy as the day before. She thought of the laundromat two blocks away with industrial-sized tumblers. Maybe she could even go for a turn herself and dry out her waterlogged brain. Something potent in this suggestion finally broke the dreary spell about her. She hopped down, pulled on a pair of worn-toed boots, and waded through the marsh of her apartment to gather everything into one bundle. It lay heavy on her back, breathing more clamminess down her neck. As she clumped noisily down the wooden staircase, a voice echoed up from the landing below.

"Alps...blanket...snow," the syllables bounced in the drafty stairwell. She tried to distinguish the foreign brogue she had heard earlier that morning, but it must have been someone further down. This enviable person, whoever it was, seemed to be recounting an early ski escapade. But the three words that Claire caught were like an arrangement of dots for connecting and filling in at will. Which, of course, she did. The resulting image was too bright and wonderful to believe, though she did for a short moment. She imagined herself boarding the next train east into the mountains, where a white powder of considerable volume and heft could fill in an entire valley, cover and hush her into a deep sleep.

Ridiculous. She cursed the reality that suddenly crashed through the brilliant ice castle and brought it shattering to the ground. *What makes me think I can afford a holiday*, she muttered under her breath. *I have nothing but a few greasy coins in my pocket, and even those should be going for a half-baguette rather than hot air.* She entered the laundromat and saw that the dryers were full, and the washing machines were still. The warm and dry air that enveloped Claire was so inviting, she didn't mind the wait. Instead, she let out a small smile at the change of climate, so welcome and unexpected, pulled the little notebook out of her pocket, and tried to put her bright surroundings into words.

***

Heaving the door open, I immediately feel the heady, sweet sigh of desert air. The dryers whine like the wind through a narrow fissure in a canyon, and long tubes of light

5

that blaze above burn as unrelenting as the unshaded sun, though strangely cool. I take a seat on a rock nearby several delicate sprigs of color — lilac, pale yellow, and white — giving off their pungent fragrance. Out of the corner of my eye, rows of black and brown tumbleweeds turn over and over. I look down and finger the edges of my book, crinkled from the time I forgot it next to an open window during a rainstorm. I had to painstakingly spread each page out hour-by-hour to save it. This is my life. Drenched in an instant, taking a patient eternity to restore.

***

Claire capped her pen as one of the machines gave off a final high-pitched wheeze. She rose and eagerly began muscling a mass of wet clothing towards the gaping hole.

"*Excusez-moi, mademoiselle.*" She started and looked over. Two small black eyes met hers with a glare which clearly snapped their intent. She was fairly certain this petite woman had arrived several minutes after her, but as she had no clear recollection during the time the book had been open, she had no way of proving anything. As usual, the written word had spirited her away and betrayed her. She was about to capitulate, when she suddenly decided to defend herself.

"*Oui, madame. C'est vrai.* I was here before you."

The woman stared her down.

"*Mais non,* you are mistaken, *mademoiselle.* I have been waiting in line for at least forty-five minutes. It is not possible that you have been here this whole time." Claire thought about it, and decided to make a fuss. She was bored. What else was there to do? She was about to muster up the most indignant and condescending French she could think up to match the woman's stance, when her eyes locked into another pair of eyes, wistful, on the other side of the glass of the laundromat window. They belonged to the man from downstairs. Suddenly, she felt sheepish about her petty insistence, and mumbled something of an apologetic surrender to the woman with the black eyes. She thought she saw the man smile, but as usual, these things were mostly hidden with him. He turned down the narrow passageway that let in the light ahead from the boulevard, and she leaned her forehead on the window. As she squinted through the steam of her breath, Claire could just barely make out the level line of his dark winter coat as it continued its daily stroll through the *quartier.* She traced that line with her finger on the window, daydreaming.

Twenty minutes later, she plunged her hands into her laundry sack. The manual action of pulling and pushing the rough wet garments was satisfying. *This is something I can cross off my to-do list. Laundry, check. Review notes for test, check. Buy bread, check. Writing . . . what exactly? What was the point?* She put the coins in the machine one-by-one and listened to them fall to the bottom. *What is significant? What is just another piece of metal rattling in a machine?* She resisted the familiar urge to run for pen and paper every time her thoughts turned philosophical. *Not everything is worth writing down.*

Neat piles of dry clothes lined up on her bed. Check. Already it was starting to clear up—the sky, the humidity, her head. As usual, everything swung together in one spectacular mood, up or down, and Claire let herself go in the sovereignty of the moment. She briefly dwelt on the reality of her biology exam the next day, and decided to take a walk to the *Jardin des Plantes*, with her tired graph-paper notes stuffed under one arm. Something alive must be out there, something that had been enticed out of the crackly brown grass by the constant dribble from the clouds over the past few weeks. Halfway down the boulevard, her hungry eyes alighted on the vivid green of a park bench, mottled layers of blue paint underneath. The garden still stretched a fair way down the slope of the avenue, and she found herself suddenly arrested by intense thought. This time, memories. The eternal present mingling with the imperfect.

***

Nature walks with my big brother Peter. Pulling on our rain boots — where's my hat? A small backpack with all of the essentials. What is essential? A compass, binoculars (Dad's pair hanging heavy around my neck), snacks for survival, small jars and plastic bags, the ubiquitous notebook. We brought the jars and the notebook empty, in hopes of bringing them back full. Rows of specimens, collected and labeled with care. Our precision must have rivaled that of the great laboratories. Now I stare at each of these details one by one, examining them with a pocket magnifying glass. My life, a collection of tiny particulars. I used to follow those tall, broad shoulders through the marsh. I'm still squatting in the mud, dried rushes rustling above. But where are you Peter?

***

She finished the last few hundred yards to the *jardin*, letting her fingers touch the rough spindles of the iron gate, painted over with more gleaming black to cover up the rust. She paused at the model of the small stegosaurus outside the Museum of Natural History adjacent to the garden. It always made her smile to see this ancient creature standing defiantly in the foreground of perfect rows of plane trees and manicured herb gardens- a funny mixture of scientific order and wild, unbridled eras of prehistory. Science really was a work of the imagination. This elevated Claire's spirits considerably, and she turned towards the length of the park stretched out before her, when a voice behind made her jump.

"How they thought up that creature from a pile of bones, beyond me." Claire turned and saw her neighbor leaning on his cane, his gray beard pointing skeptically at the statue in front of both of them.

"Sir, you find it ridiculous?"

"In my time, we could identify each bone precisely within minutes with nothing more than a reference book, counting the occurrences in each square meter, measuring– the young folk these days with their computer simulations and what have you—they have no idea . . ."

"I love to count."

"Eh? Oh well, good. *Tant mieux*." Claire still could not place his accent, nor stifle her curiosity any longer.

"Sir, may I ask where you are from?

"Do you count bones, then?" he asked, ignoring her question.

"No...no, I am studying microbiology—er—specifically in the Camargue region."

"Humph. What are you doing here?" Claire felt her cheeks getting warm with the incessant queries—and the ambiguity of this last one. She had not been obliged to explain herself to anyone for months, and had rather forgotten how.

"Sir, I—"

"My name is Arthur—Art."

"Okay . . . Art. I am doing a *stage* here at the *Institut Pasteur*."

"Oh, well. That's good enough, I guess." Claire meant to hide her disappointment at his dismissive tone, but must have failed, for he cocked an eye in her direction from under his ever-impressive brow, and added, "I suppose you like that, then?" *Like it. Well, yes.* She turned in the direction of the stately building and opened her mouth to respond, but he interrupted her again:

"I walk past those doors every day—part of my morning constitutional."

"Why?" Her little word seemed rather bare and inquisitive, like a sharp scalpel, but it was too late to draw it back.

"Habit. I used to work across the garden, here." Art turned slowly on his heel, poked with his cane at the chalky sand, and shifted his weight. "But now I'm the dinosaur." He guffawed loudly, immensely enjoying the joke at his own expense. Claire smiled politely but dared no more. After his shoulders stopped shaking in leftover laughter, he nodded to her as if they were simply passing in the street, and continued his stroll across the shadow lines of the bare, leafless trees. He never had mentioned where he had come from, or where he was going.

That evening, she ran a dull peeler over a few tired, rubbery carrots, hoping to revive them in yet another bowl of couscous. *He's worked in my lab? He walks past every day! How could this be the first time I've seen him?* Claire shivered. Maybe he was the ghost of some former, misunderstood biologist, nervously floating through the gardens and halls, still vying for a long-lost peer review of a research paper. But seriously. She and Art had lived not eight feet apart for four months, only rarely crossing paths, never once exchanging words. Now, he kept appearing out of nowhere and thoroughly haunted her thoughts. She set the water to boil and grabbed her notebook, anxious to record the course of events, to better understand them, to give bodies to the phantoms wandering in and out of her brain.

***

Sometimes words are like points plotted out on a graph, only in laying them out can I find the needful pattern. Pin them down. Push the pins in all the way. But Peter, my thumb hurts when I do that. His big, calloused hands were better suited to the task. We were hanging maps of the stars on the ceiling of my bedroom. I remember he promised me I could put glow-in-the-dark stars up for every constellation I learned to identify. I love to count, he said. I will count them all someday. And I believed he would, his curly-headed silhouette thrust into the starry sky. But I will spend my days with gaze downwards, bowed down like a broken reed in these endless winter marshes.

***

She frowned, dissatisfied. *Nothing of this man will make sense for me.* Claire meant, of course, Arthur, but it could have gone for brother, neighbor, friend. An image which often haunted her leaped again to her mind's eye. She remembered lying in her bed as a girl, when she would turn from the still-unfinished constellations glowing in weird, artificial green-white points on the ceiling to the real skyline outside. Without exception, like a ritual, her eyes were drawn each night to the gnarled tree across the street. The black trunk halfway up clearly cut the shape of a strong man, his broad upper arms reaching out and up to cover and protect. As long as she could catch a glimpse of him, she was able to fall asleep. Claire curled up on her futon and pinched her eyes shut, hoping to conjure up that same image, and the effect. But instead, all she could see were the square shoulders of a dark winter coat walking away. As she drifted off, she half-believed that it was Peter.

By the time the next morning's sun came spilling onto the chilly gray cement floors of the lab, Claire had already been hunched over her microscope for an hour and a half. Her eyes were dry, and as she blinked, the water from her eyes puddled up on the eyepiece. *Why I even bothered to put on mascara this morning.* She wiped the water stains from under her eyes and the eyepiece and perched again over the tiny murky spot under the bright lights. The small collection of specimens looked like Scorpio in the sky but a reverse image—black on white instead of white on black. *Like words on a page*, she thought idly. With one hand, she worked the focus dial, and with the other she sketched the amoebae that writhed and floated under her watchful eye. *How strange for them. Always under surveillance.* Claire had always felt an odd mix of empathy and jealousy for anything kept under watch. *Just one more sketch.*

Suddenly, everything went dark. Claire's head popped up, only to see Hugo, her lab partner, grinning stupidly across from her, his elbows propped up on the well-worn, black work bench between them.

"Hugo, stop it. What is your problem?" She wanted her tone to convey just how juvenile she thought he was in general, regardless of the present form of trouble he was creating.

"*Regarde.*"

"*Quoi?*" She looked down, and saw the white of an envelope out of the corner of her eye. She snatched it from the counter, and was about to lecture him about interrupting her experiments with lesser matters, when her eyes fell on the return address. She stuffed it in the pocket of her lab coat with a pair of lab scissors and made Hugo promise to guard her microscope till she came back.

Rushing past the coffee machine, Claire ducked into the toilet room and wedged herself in one of the stalls. She took out the scissors and methodically inserted the point under the glue to gently pry the flap open. Mom had finally sent her something. As she unfolded the paper in her hand, she saw portions of text in her own scrawl, rather than her mother's.

***

Today Peter went to university. I knew that the house would seem empty, but I didn't realize it would be so sudden, so quiet. He left me most of his books, and just seeing them makes me sick. I cannot even look at The Amateur Naturalist. *It was our favorite . . .*

We got a letter from Peter today, and he loves everything...

He does not write anymore. He is really busy when we call him. Of course he is! He's smart and wants to study . . . .

We haven't heard from him in weeks, and the line is always busy.

He met someone named . . .

***

15

Claire stopped reading, as the words swam in front of her in blurs, like a landscape of unfocused specimens that she could not bring into clarity. It was overwhelming. The large globules of tears forming in her eyes overflowed, staining her white lab coat with the rest of her makeup. Black on white, the story was already written out. She was not ready to reread it.

Returning to the lab, she fingered the envelope, slowly took it out of her pocket again and placed it under the microscope, adjusting the light to shine above. So magnified, the curves, lines and dots on the paper fibers took on the appearance of tiny mountain ranges, surrounded by snow-covered prairies. Claire lost herself in the details and found solace. Maybe someday she would be able to turn the knob back up and look at the greater signification, but for now this was enough.

Her peripheral vision suddenly caught a quick motion, and she peeked up to meet a pair of bright eyes. They were set deep in the tousled, rumpled figure of the perpetually harried grad student from across the hallway. Eliot tried to cover for his unexpected arrival in the flippant yet formal English of his native Cambridge:

"Say, is there anyone about?"

Claire blinked twice. Her stark face, still splotched from the storm of tears, wrote some kind of story, apparent but unexplained.

"Er—sorry. I'll come back another time," as the young man realized his intrusion. His head hung for an apologetic moment in the doorway, then disappeared, pulling Claire's heart along with him. She was genuinely surprised. Where was he taking it? Once he was gone, she walked over to the deep sinks and dabbed her face with some cool water. She leaned on the clammy ceramic for a moment, sighed, and ventured towards his desk.

When she entered the room, she first saw his broad, lanky shoulders, hunched over a spaghetti-like pile of black cords. He whistled softly to himself as he tried to untangle them, as if to charm half a dozen serpents into submission with his song.

"Hi." Claire stated.

He jumped, ran a hand quickly over his head—a gesture that seemed common enough to him, given his wild mop of hair—and stammered:

"Well, hi. Say, really sorry I barged in—"

"No!" Claire calmed her tone. "No, it's all right. I just received something from home, and you know, it's hard to—to be away." *Not exactly the truth, but close enough.*

"Right. I suppose you have a lot of friends over there," he offered.

"Uh, some, yeah." She lied. This was not going well. "Actually, I mainly miss my family." *That was better.*

"Sure." He visibly brightened for a moment, then scrunched his brows down in sympathy. "Yes, I can certainly relate. My family's the only real connection I have to Cambridge—except for my professors, of course." He seemed to be trying to tell her something, but she couldn't quite grasp it. "Uh, would you be willing to take a break from the lab and go and help me with a bird count? I need another person to help string up the mist nets and hold a boom mic." He let the words slide by without any further explanation, apparently inviting her to share in his code.

"Yeah, give me a minute to lock my stuff up. I'll meet you out front in five." Suddenly, she felt shy and plunged her hands deep in her lab coat pockets, her hand touching again the envelope. The memory seemed less potent now somehow, her old words a drastic exaggeration. She wanted to put them away for a very long time, perhaps forever.

"Hey—thanks," Eliot said. Claire smiled a reply and excused herself. *Thank you,* she thought.

One hour later, they were standing in the lucid sunshine of a tiny square adjacent to the *Jardin des Plantes*. Eliot explained how his research on bird songs in the city required hours of samples, and his funding was soon to run out. Desperate for a hand, he had stopped by to see if anyone in the other departments was available. Claire found herself thrusting a microphone towards the irregular, pale-blue patches of sky, overlaid by the black, lacy tree crowns. It vaguely reminded her of the images in her petri dish, the live bacteria spreading its delicate fingers through a tiny, round globe. It was stunning.

"Hey, can you hold that mic any higher up?"

***

I can hold it nearly high as the trees, at least on tiptoe. I will capture these sounds and keep them for myself. I will record every twist and turn of these warbling voices — the birds' and yours. Hold it, hold it . . . there! Sh, now. The trick is to get the mic up there slowly without spooking 'em. But what if the wind carries the songs away? The wind carried Peter's songs away all of the time. I listen as hard as I can, cupping a hand around an ear to collect the smallest sounds ahead. Hee-hoo. The heart leaps at the sound so near. I press the record button and let it roll.

***

Later that evening, Claire leaned on the radiator in her apartment, now cool to the touch. Art's dehumidifier sat in the corner, quiet and still. She had to remember to bring that back to him one of these days. *What would Art think of Eliot?* She felt the need to tell someone, someone other than the little book. She was about to reach for her journal, out of habit, when her musings were interrupted by the swish of a paper

19

slipped under the door. Puzzled, Claire walked carefully towards the bright square of white and peered at it, wondered what it could mean. She bent over to pick it up, and opening it, her eyes fell upon a small gathering of old-fashioned script:

> *You are invited to Sunday brunch*
> *Tomorrow, my place, one o'clock p.m.*
> *Bring a friend if you like.*
> *Art.*

Claire's eyebrows moved progressively higher with each line, as she marveled at the ancient gentleman's offer. *What an odd thing to do.* The greater surprise was that it did not make Claire feel strange. No, this was a welcome change. The past few months had been a dreary string of solitary hours, an email inbox full of nothing but spam, and suppers eaten over her textbooks. Her best conversations to date had been with the woman from whom she bought her half-baguette every evening, the old man who lived downstairs, Hugo when he bothered her, and her faithful journal.

Now, a flurry of written words from the past and present flew in from all directions and settled over her, like a migratory pattern she did not yet understand. This seemingly random collection of images came swiftly from the four winds of the globe, replacing her own stale set of present-day thoughts. She impulsively grabbed her journal from the table, and taped Art's invitation on a fresh page. Suddenly, she recalled the journal fragments, still tear-stained and hidden away. Was there a home for these words, too? She leaned back, reached into the closet and pulled out a small packet of papers, a pair of scissors and a glue stick. *My life*, she thought, *a collection of wandering words.*

The following morning, Claire cracked her eyes open. Groggy, in her clothes from the night before, she glimpsed an empty wine glass with a red stain in the bottom balanced on a pile of books next to the futon. Ribbons of white and irregular shapes of text scattered around like a bizarre snowfall. Her journal lay cocked half-open, dropped at some unknown, exhausted hour. She peered inside—yes, some of the scraps had found their way in. Curlicues of scribbled commentary wound around the patches of text, an attempt at reconciliation of past and present. Parenthetical, perhaps. But not trivial.

***

(Christmas at home, 10 years ago now.) Disaster. That girl Peter brought sat on the couch most of the day, one thin leg crossed over and under the other, flipping through the same three copies of the New Yorker, looking bored and annoyed at Pete every once in a while. He seems okay. (In love with an image.) He acts like it's cute, the way her tiny ivory hands

21

refuse to do the dishes, much less give a hand hauling the Christmas tree. "Ooh, noo. I don't want to get in the way." Give me a break. Pete just laughs and said, "Step aside, it's man's work anyway." I already had my hands wrapped fully around the trunk, sap and all.

Just now, she takes out a file and starting fussing over her nails for — the twelfth time, I think. She does it every time mom comes in to invite her into the kitchen. She's completely oblivious to dad's attempts at conversation, too — he retreated into the woodshop a long time ago to finish some Christmas gift or another. I should go keep him company.

(The conversation I heard when I left the room.) "Is there anything to do in this town, for God's sake, P?" She hisses. Nervous silence. I peek around the corner, and his shoulders are drooping. She calls him "P," of all things.

Where did my strong Peter go?

***

Claire rolled off the couch and peeled off her jeans and stale shirt for a shower. She found the note from Art in the mess and glanced up at the clock. *I may as well make an effort, bring out the respectable Sunday best.* She didn't have a skirt, but navy slacks would do. A scarf and earrings would dress it up a bit. Workdays in the lab did not usually include such finicky details, but as she glanced in the mirror one more time to finger-comb her bangs, she realized that it might not hurt occasionally.

She walked carefully down to Art's doorway in her one pair of heels, worn and painful, paused and then rapped on his door. The sound her knuckles made on the glossy blue painted door frame echoed throughout the building, and she suddenly felt self-conscious. Art's door opened a long moment later and rescued her from the eyes of the neighbors. They probably didn't care anyway.

"*Salut.* You can leave your shoes on or take 'em off. I've got the tea kettle on." He turned abruptly back down the narrow hallway, barely wide enough for two pairs of shoes side-by-side. She thanked him, took her pumps off gratefully and followed the shaft of light glancing off of his broad shoulders. He hobbled slightly, so that golden beams of dust danced off his back with tick-tock regularity.

Heading directly into the sunlight, she couldn't see right away, but soon her eyes adjusted and the shadowy blues and browns of her surroundings sharpened into detail after detail. There were burgeoning bookshelves on every available wall, from the overlapped, worn oriental rugs on the floor all the way up the vaulted ceilings. Other shapes appeared then, adorning the side-tables and edges of the shelves—spiral fossils, coal imprinted with ferns, photos of expeditions. *Like a museum of his life.* Claire kept these observations to herself while they exchanged fits and starts of conversation about the weather, the state of the current worker's strike, and how the coin-op laundry would soon be going from 4 euros a load to 4.50.

"Scandalous, I tell you. When I moved here as a young student, we paid no more than 50 centimes for washin' an' dryin'." He finished this observation with the disgruntled clang of a wooden spoon on cast iron.

Claire was tickled to realize that this man who had seemed so curmudgeonly at first was beginning to show his friendly side. *There must be something about being on his own plot of land that puts him at ease.* Claire was in the process of trying to think whether such a place in the world even existed where she felt like that, when he addressed her directly:

"Here I am, carryin' on. *Alors ma chercheuse,* what tales have you from the laboratory these days?" He looked at her pointedly for an answer.

"Well, I-I've been working on a particular set of sodium structures found in the salt marshes in the *Sud,* and what affect they have on bacteria growing in that area." She offered her stock response, lightly sprinkled with science. Art grabbed an enormous mortar and pestle with one hand and it landed on the table in front of him with a dull thud.

"I always use salt from the Camargue, you know. It's fabulous on soft-boiled eggs." He sighed. "Alas, my expertise in sodiums pretty much ends with my forays into cuisine. But calcium—now there, we can talk."

They spent the next hour talking fossils and bones over good English tea, buttered toast, and eggs, and thick-sliced bacon. Claire leaned back, happy and satisfied. At that moment, she caught a glimpse of a photograph of a pretty brunette, gracefully aged, and ventured a question.

"Is that your wife?"

"That's my Mollie, mine for about 35 years, till this world couldn't hold her anymore. I've been somehow gettin' by on my own for fifteen years now, though I don't quite see how." A shadow passed over his eyes which had been dancing most of the morning.

"Art, I'm sorry. She was beautiful."

"Aye." He paused. "Well, I suppose it's about time to get going, eh?"

Claire felt terrible. She had obviously brought up something painful, and that after his many kindnesses. Embarrassed, she got up from her chair and stuck out her hand to shake his.

"I had a really wonderful time, *merci,* Art."

"*Mais oui.* I hope you come again—maybe next week?" He offered.

"Oh!" She was truly surprised that she hadn't alienated him with her nosiness. "I'll let you know, thanks." As Claire mounted the steps back to her place, she thought about the school project she had to finish translating into French, and yawned wearily. Translating the past into the present had taken all of her strength.

***

The next morning, Claire turned on her machine in the lab, pulled out a box of fresh, empty glass slides, and set herself to work. Taking the first one, she paused. Was this Hugo's idea of another joke, messing up her experiments? A label had been carefully placed in the center of the slide, rather than along the side, and contained lettering too small for Claire's myopic vision. On a whim, she stuck it under the microscope, carefully eying around her, to make sure no one was watching. Her brow furrowed above the eyepiece in puzzlement when she saw neat, unfamiliar typing, arranged in a series of short phrases, as straight and measured as Orion's belt:

Hunt. *Songs.* *With me.*

Claire's thoughts swooped like swallows, diving into images from the previous day in the park with Eliot. She recalled how they had walked along the straight line of plane trees, while he delved into the details of his project. At one point, he motioned for her to follow him and approach the tall screens of green gauze that covered entire length of the fence on one edge of the garden.

"Can you guess?"

26

"Privacy?" Claire joked.

"Not too far off. It fools the birds into thinking that no one's there, so they stay and sing." Eliot looked at her—*in a funny way,* now that she thought about it. "We'll find ourselves a perch just underneath." They had scrunched down, side-by-side, backs to the fence, while he taught her how to recognize the voices of the unabashed birds—the magpie, the crow, the blackbird. Claire did not tell him that Peter had taught her these songs long ago. She sat quietly, her knees pulled up to her chest, and let his murmur rise and fall, weaving in and out of the bird calls. She dared not speak.

***

I'm quivering on the inside, my breath on vibrate. New life implanted like a nervous word lodged in my throat. How can I sing like you, carefree one? I know. Put me behind the gauzy green of a blind, and I could sing anything. But not here, now. I cannot open my giddy mouth in your glowing presence, for fear of the flutter bursting out into the open. I am a timid one, but please don't give up on me. Take me, record me, hunt songs of me.

***

Late that night, crouched down with her back pressed against the iron bars of the park, Claire clicked

27

the flashlight on, then off. On, then off. Long, short, short long. She waited, told the muscles in her shoulders to relax. The response came, like a lightning bug, minuscule and urgent, spelling out a constellation of meaning: C-E-D-R-U-S L-I-B-A-N-I. They would meet under the cedar of Lebanon. Once, Claire had walked past that venerated tree, and was amused to find a woman with her arms wrapped around it. She just stood there, her eyes closed in an expression of perfect serenity. Somehow Claire had understood.

She crept through the shadows of the flora she knew so well, those old friends with their long, Latin names. Soon she would be past the greenhouse, ghostly in the moonlight, and in the next stand of trees. *The trysting place.* She blushed in the dark. A rustle in the brush caught her ear and she cocked her head to check for a familiar profile. Must have been an owl, or a night vole. Then she heard the call of a nightingale, perfect. Too perfect. She reached the clearing, and walked tentatively towards the source of the song.

Hey.

Hey, he brushed her right and left cheeks with his. She waited with her heart on tiptoe, but a third kiss never came. Their eyeglasses clinked.

He backed up a bit awkwardly and looked her up and down, dressed in the dark-green coveralls of an official gardener, the same pair that had hung abandoned in the lab closet for as long as anyone could remember. *He said to wear dark clothing.* She saw his shoulders moving up and down in suppressed laughter, and the uneasiness between them broke. He extended his hand and she almost took it. *Silly Claire.* He was simply offering to help with the heavy equipment slung around her neck: recording device, microphone, camera. She nodded silently and handed the bulk of the weight to him. *This is just a research trip, right?* In fact, it would be a clandestine mission, since his approval to be in the garden hadn't officially come through yet. Eliot's time was short, and still many songs to capture before his return to England. Claire didn't want to think about it.

They spent about an hour and a half of ducking in and out of shadowy moonlight, trapping the coos and quavers of the nocturnal inhabitants of the trees. Claire rubbed the tiredness out of her eyes, when Eliot hissed a warning:

"Look out—guard at 3 o'clock." They slid into the labyrinth of bushes leading up to the highest point in the park, crowned with a diminutive platform tower that resembled a bird cage. They waited until the capped silhouette paused, then turned on his heel and went his way, whistling.

"He's a good whistler." Eliot noted. "Humph. Let's go to the top, just for fun. Don't worry—there's enough cover with the shrubs." Claire nodded her reply, and they began the climb. After ten minutes of muffled chuckles through the maze of hedges with false turns and trick paths, they finally reached the top. In the stillness of the circular structure, Claire scuffed at the worn marble with her shoe, and wondered how many lovers had found themselves there. "A + K." "*Guillaume aime Pernette.*" The stones told stories, albeit youthful ones. Eliot had his back to her, and his tall, square frame melded with the Cedar of Lebanon, now far in the distance. In spite of herself, Claire gasped. *It was him—the man in the tree. He was him.* Eliot flipped around.

"Wha?" He queried, dropping the final "t" as usual.

"Euh. Hmm. Nice night, huh?" Claire struggled to sequester her girlish fantasies to the past and focus on the now.

"What's the matter?" She gave a quick cheerful shrug that meant *forget it* and sat down on the smooth bench that encircled the inside of the lookout. *Close call. He probably already thinks I'm crazy.* Eliot sat down next to her, his hands grasping the seat on either side of his knees, his shoulders hunched up.

"I have a confession to make," he stated. Claire froze.

"I've been a dreadful sham. Actually, it's more about-" He leaned over and brushed her cheek with his lips. First the right, then the left, then drifted carefully to

30

her mouth. They both waited there a long moment—stars singing or birds shining? Hard to tell when the golden glow of the city diffused all their natural observations into one glory moment.

She was about to reach for his hand, when he backed up, a slight wrinkle of anguish in his forehead. "Damn. I—I was only going to ask you something."

"What is it, Eliot?" Her new trust started to wobble inside.

"I'm terrible. I need to let you alone, you've got connections back home. I—"

"What?" She was genuinely surprised.

"You get those letters from back home. Hugo told me." He looked at her again and shrugged hopelessly. "Sorry." The letters . . . the last one came flashing in front of her eyes. Claire couldn't move or talk, everything was happening too fast for her explain. It was like a dream where she wanted to run or scream, but couldn't, frozen in place. In the void, Eliot continued with an embarrassed look:

"You don't have to say anything. I'm an ass, and I know it. You can expect me to respect your privacy from now on." And with these words, he slipped back into his formal self—more distant, professional. She pleaded inwardly. *No. Don't leave me.* But all she could do was look at him, slack-jawed.

31

"Please excuse me for keeping you out so late." His transformation back into the polite Cambridge fellow that Claire knew from the laboratory was abrupt. Claire searched inwardly, desperately, for a way to explain, but it seemed too late. She would have to wait for another opportunity. They quietly worked their way down the hill and through the back gate without another word, parting ways on the street with a quick nod and *ciao*.

***

With heavy but sleepless eyes, Claire laid on her back in bed and replayed the evening's events, by now a tired cycle. Hope and disappointment clashed and came crashing together in the moment in the towering rotunda. Why hadn't she explained? She tried with all her might to think objectively, employ her keen powers of observation. She examined every angle, tried to trace the pattern. Peter always said your eyes were stronger on the periphery. *If you look at the sky indirectly, you might see something not normally visible to the naked eye.* Finally, as if on the outskirts of her inner vision, she felt a flicker of recognition. It grew slowly and licked around the edges, a smoldering flame melting the glossy photograph from the outside in. But could she make out the image before it disappeared?

***

You want to see the structure inside the cell, you know what you gotta do? I prop my elbows high on a long workbench in the musty garden shed. Stain the slide, like this one. He holds a tinted rectangular window to my eye, turning my whole world rosy. Hey Pete, can I do it? He takes another square of cover glass, minuscule, paper-thin compared to the slide. Hey! Stop that. They're fragile, stupid. You have to hold them on the edges, but don't squeeze. Yeah, like that. I'll grab the stain. He turns his back, and the little window crumbles in my hand, shards in small fingers. It feels like splinters — oo! He turns, sees the glass below me covered in red. I didn't mean to, Pete. Sobbing. His terrible, grim silence. The emergency room, where he wouldn't even look at me. This tiny life, an isolated globule. And these irrevocable stains.

***

Claire sat bolt upright, fumbled through the dust to the switch of the floor lamp. *Stupid?* Did he really say that? She tried to remember when her elbows would have reached Peter's tall desk in the lab. Age nine? Curiosity overcame her apprehension, and she scrambled over to the shoe box in the closet, taking out handfuls of paper scraps. On the bottom was an unopened letter, addressed to Claire Sivert. The return address just said "Sivert," but Claire knew exactly who it was from. It was a girl she did not know but who shared her last name, that mysterious person who Peter had married and divorced within a year. This had to be from sometime near the end of their relationship, she thought. The lacy postmark was the only evidence for the couple of years that the missive had remained sealed. Now, the wrench of a dull knife through the flap, and soon more truth spilled into the open for her to mourn.

> *Dear Claire,*
>
> *I know that we don't know each other that well, but I needed someone to talk to who might understand. Peter has become increasingly unreasonable and threatening over the past few months. Even — well, you can tell this to no one, and hide this letter, but he's hit me three times. You do not believe me. There is no way that you could. You think the world of him. I did too. But you don't know what he's like when you're not around.*
>
> *Please call.*
>
> *Mary*

Claire put a hand to her face to daub her cheeks, now wet with tears. The voice of one crying for help, and she had never thought to read it. But it was the final sentence, awful in its ambiguity, that made her sadness swell. *You don't know what he's like when you're not around.* An echo of her own battered warble, the phrase verbatim when Claire had tried to tell Dad. But like Peter said, there's nothing worse than a tattletale. She laid the words on the table believing them and collapsed into bed, exhausted from the remembering.

***

The next morning, Claire ambled down the stairs, closing the door on the mess of laundry and dishes in the apartment. She was equally happy to forget about her journal, at least for a while. Seeing it on the table only reminded her of the agonized lettering inscribed inside, lists of questions that she would ask Eliot—or Peter—if she ever got the chance. She was also beginning to find her own gloomy company tiresome, and was grateful to be heading to Art's place for a change of scenery. She tapped on the familiar blue door.

"C'mon in, it's open!" A powerful, growly voice emanated through the thick oak. Sunday mornings at Art's had become a weekly ritual. *Like family.* She slipped off her flats and walked into the warm glow of crepes and coffee.

"Ah!" His eyes brightened as she came around the corner. "*Comment vas-tu, ma chère?*" Seeing the dark circles under her eyes, he frowned. "Humph. We'll get

35

you right as rain as soon as I can get you sittin' down and eatin' some breakfast."

"Thanks, Art. Just haven't been sleeping all that well." He grunted, finding her response obvious but unsatisfactory.

"Well, I'll let you set the table anyway—not too tired for that, I hope?"

"No, certainly not," she laughed. Tugging at the hefty silverware drawer, she took out forks and knives, straightened the plates and napkins. A few minutes later, he looked over approvingly.

"Looks real nice the way you've got the table. Reminds me of how Mollie used to do it, though all her fussin' was a little beyond me at the time. Miss it now." Claire thought she saw him wince a bit, but he turned away too quickly to the stove. When he came around again, he had a twinkle in his eye.

"Let's sit down, then." They each took their places at the end of Art's broad, heavy table, piled on the other side with books and journals. After exchanging a quick *"bon ap',"* they spent a few minutes of contented humming over the delicate crepes and homemade peach compote.

"I've got a theory about your unusually soporific state, my young friend," pointing to her weary head propped up on her hand next to her plate. Embarrassed by her manners, she straightened herself, remembering suddenly to put the woven cloth napkin on her lap.

"I think you'd got yourself a *beau*," he gleamed triumphantly. Perhaps it was the little old-fashioned word. Or its true meaning in the French. Maybe the touch of Irish whiskey in her coffee. In any case, Claire turned beet red from the scalloped collar of her flowered blouse all the way up to her hairline.

"Art, really, I don't know where you—er—got that idea." Meanwhile, her abashed response clearly betrayed her.

"Indeed, a human being—not to mention a scientist—doesn't get to my stage in life without learning how to make a risky hypothesis here and there. I had ta' do such a thing when I started thinkin' about my Mollie, for example." Finally he confessed. "Nay, I saw you two walkin' in the garden." He looked at her knowingly. "I wasn't born yesterday. Obviously." Claire's mind dove back as she thought hard about when that would have been, what that would have been. She wanted to ask him a thousand questions about that moment, to reconstruct the past, so recent and yet so difficult to remember.

"I—er, hm. I'd rather not talk about it," she faltered.

"I can respect that, little miss. However-" He leaned in. "Given your line o' work, he'd better be worth his salt." Completely overcome by his own joke, he laughed until the tears ran down his cheeks. After wiping his eyes with an enormous blue handkerchief, he looked up and saw real distress in her drawn face. Letting out a long whistle through his teeth, he leaned back and looked at her with steady, gray-eyed honesty and said:

"He'd better be worth *you*. Or I'll have something to say about it." With that, he thumped his napkin on the table, hoisted himself out of his chair, and wandered down the hallway to his room, muttering something about getting ready for his *promenade*.

Claire was momentarily relieved to be left alone and recover a bit from Art's interrogation. She shook herself up, and approached one of the many bookshelves lining the *salon*. Running her finger along the dusty edge, she scanned the crumbling leather spines of dozens of books, mostly scientific in scope. *Histoire de la Paléontologie, Bones of the Northern Country, Rêveries d'un Promeneur Solitaire.* She paused at the last one, so slim, nearly hidden in the tight space between broader tomes. She cocked her head. *The Reveries of the Solitary Walker. A bit philosophical for practical Art, no?* She carefully wiggled it out, and the marbled covers with faded red leather corners parted easily, opening to the first promenade:

> I am now alone on earth, no longer
> having any brother, neighbor, friend,
> or society other than myself.

38

The intense solitude that permeated the page ran through her too, her eyes transfixed by the words "friend," "brother," until she tore them away, finding refuge a few paragraphs further down:

> The leisurely moments of my daily walks have often been filled with charming periods of contemplation which I regret having forgotten. I will set down in writing those which still come to me and each time I reread them I will enjoy them anew . . . these pages . . . only a shapeless diary.

If only her memories were so light and airy, made her forget her trials. She shuddered at the thought of someone else reading the dark thoughts that she had recently fixed in her own journal. *Shapeless diary,* indeed. Art's footfall came creaking down the hallway, and he caught sight of her with the book.

"Eh? You found my Rousseau. You're too young to understand that one, *ma petite.*" She decided to amuse him with a sliver of defiance.

"Actually, I think I find myself more cynical than he," she countered.

"Now, that's a true shame, at your tender age." He eyed her, then shook his head. "Nay, you might fancy yourself a bitter old woman, but you're young yet.

Read the passage on the autumn of life, and then tell me you belong in the ranks of the *troisième age*." Claire nodded solemnly as if accepting the challenge and began to leaf through the yellowed pages again.

"A walk, then?" He invited her with a chuckle.

"Yes, I'll go with you partway." She slipped the *Rêveries* in her coat pocket, grabbed her hat, and they were off.

***

As Art and Claire walked down the boulevard, she wondered silently what the passing figures bent under the gray skies must think of them. A grandfather and his granddaughter? A kind social worker and her charge? Who is caring for whom? The wind spitefully kicked up dark, bedraggled leaves, bits of decay and autumnal melancholy turned up on what might have been a spring day. *What might have been.* The blank slate of sky promised no star-gazing that evening. As they strolled by, Claire's eyes rested for the hundredth time on a poster plastered to the wall next to the imprinted "*Défense d'Afficher.*" The colorful rectangle advertised a special evening in *Parc Montsouris* "under the stars." Claire had hoped this would be intriguing to Eliot, though he seemed to prefer chasing birds. She wanted to reach out somehow, explain that everything was fine. *Not that you can see much of the sky in this city,* she

40

concluded, hanging her head. The day, begun so hopeful, had grown dreary. Art and Claire had unwittingly missed their opportunity that golden morning for a pleasant stroll. *Oh, right . . . Art.*

"Thanks for the book." Kind words seemed stilted and forced in the dreariness, but she had just enough in her to make the reach.

"Aye." Art seemed just as pensive as she.

Claire slid her hand past the satin lining of her wool coat, feeling the hard edges of the thin book nestled in the corners of her pocket.

"This is all Rousseau's fault, you know?" She gestured with her free hand, as if to include the antique leaves clinging to dead branches, the four-toned landscape, the sad sameness of the street.

"How do you figure that?" His curt remark awoke them both into the reality of the vibrancy of the day. The wind became invigorating rather than something to fight. She tried to explain herself.

"Well, it's like you were saying about the autumn of life. It's hardly the season. I mean, we're coming on to the springtime. I've been cataloging signs of spring in my journal for three weeks already." Her face warmed a little, and she turned away sheepishly. "It's a habit I've had since I was a little girl. You know, phenology."

"Now, how about that." His cane paused, and he stood on the corner just before the *Jardin des Plantes*.

"That's a fine idea. Let's look for some today." Caught up in sudden, youthful zeal, he whipped the point of his cane to the left and indicated a bus on the other side of the road. "Run and catch 'em, will you, young legs? Hold the vehicle and tell 'im you've got an old geezer to take care of."

Claire rolled her eyes and took off to flag down the driver before he disappeared further down the river. Boarding the bus together, they worked their way to the back. A teenager with ear buds, despite an insolent slouch, quickly popped out of the worn seat near the door and cocked his oversized white cap in Art's direction.

"*Merci,*" he nodded gratefully, and grunted as he sat down. "Ok, Claire." He spoke to her in French to disappear into the crowd. "The place to look for springtime is . . . can you guess?"

She laid out a map of the city in her head, and flew over it, trying to pinpoint the best location. "*Buttes Chaumont?*"

"Aye, that'd be nice. But my bones are too tired to go that far." He paused. "I was thinking of Luxembourg. It's downright busy on a Sunday, and I hate the miniature horses they bring in for the kids, but today's windy enough to blow off the smell. And most of the people," he snickered. It reminded Claire how cantankerous her friend could be when he tried, and she felt a secret satisfaction in having worked her way into his kindness.

When they reached the stop next to the towering iron gate, the park was almost unoccupied. A few die-hard Parisians slouched in scattered green *chaises*, noses in journals and books. These would have been coveted chairs on a sunny day, but most of them were forgotten. The sharp wind blew across the bare sand, creating small dust storms—a desert and deserted.

Art and Claire began meandering along one of the curved pathways behind the trees, shielded from the stinging sand. The flower beds exhibited the latest installment from the green-coveralled gardeners employed by the city. Every few weeks, they would plant, dig up, and re-plant. The frequent shifting made them more like arranged bouquets than gardens.

"My botanist friends don't really approve of that," Claire confessed to Art. "They don't like the artificiality, prefer to stay on the scientific side of things in the *Jardin des Plantes*, you know?"

"I suppose that's true enough," said Art thoughtfully. "There's still something nice about bouquets in winter. Does our friend in your pocket have anything to say about flowers?"

Claire had forgotten about gloomy Rousseau, and was surprised that Art had brought it up. But she compliantly pulled the small volume from her coat.

43

"Try promenade seven," he said, leaning over her shoulder on his cane. She paged through the delicate, aged leaves and found where to begin.

"Plants seem to have been sown profusely on the earth, like the stars in the sky, in inviting man to the study of nature by the attraction of pleasure and curiosity . . ." She trailed off, enjoying the awe of the comparison. Stars and the green earth.

"Continue on," Art encouraged her.

"But the heavenly bodies are set far away from us. Preliminary knowledge, instruments, and very long ladders are needed to get to them and bring them within our reach." Art was stroking his chin thoughtfully, so she read further yet. "Plants are naturally within our reach. They are born under our feet and in our hands." She looked up. "Is that the part you meant?"

"Aye. That's a good one. They're meant to be spreading under our feet. Not contained in boxes, scientific or not," he concluded.

"I like the part about the stars." She felt bare saying this, as if it were some sort of confession.

"Why's that, little one?" His tone invited confidence.

"I sympathize with him. It's easier to bend down and touch the earth than reach for the stars." When this phrase crossed her lips, it was first time she had ever thought about it that way. She bent her knees to crouch and peer and the inside of a tulip, and thought about how things were beginning to come into focus. At least, clearer than they'd ever been.

***

Focus. The magnifying glass Dad gave me when I was five when still needed two fat baby hands to hang on to the heavy round head. Mom thought I was too young for a "real one," but Peter would help me with it, she'd see. I'd pass whole afternoons cross-legged in the humid grass, the round glass trained on a flower with all its delicate pistils and tendrils, waiting for insects to alight. Later, I learned how to see things smaller, deeper. Digging up samples in the marshes behind the house, and cataloging every last specimen. Pete and I had gotten a book out of the library on different species of bugs. It had taken three weeks on order for it to be brought to our small town branch, but we finally got a phone call one day telling them it had arrived. How funny to read the long names in Latin. We had always just said "sow bug", but now we felt it proper to honor God's creatures with a special, scientific title. Oniscidea. Clara and Petrus.

***

"Claire!" He was almost shouting, at least by Parisian standards. She was startled out of her reverie by Art's exclamation. A stout insect marched like an armadillo through the dirt in front of her nose.

45

"Art!" She countered. "What?"

"Just wondering whether you found anything down there, spring signs or no?"

"Oh, Art. Wait till I tell you. I'm still interpreting."

***

The holidays were nearing; the spring teased them with warmer sunbeams about every five days or so. It was a gradual coming; not the joyful explosion that came sprinting out of the deep freeze of the North Country that Claire knew best. The scaly plane trees along the boulevard still had no foliage from when they had lost it a few months earlier. Claire remembered, vividly. It had begun with a yellow stripe along the edge of each green leaf, a slow creeping inward over several weeks' time, draining that year's life from each leaf until they glowed like copper. Claire loved that moment, when death became beautiful. It was a momentary pleasure, soon passing. Soon all that remained was be the thick, odd-shaped branches; bare, knobby, arthritic hands reaching into the gray sky. Skin and bones.

Bones had been his nickname in college, Art told her last time. How funny that her best friend should be nearly four times her age. At least that's what she figured. She had become more than a little protective, even feeling strange about leaving for Manitoba for the

46

two weeks over Easter. And would Eliot miss her? He probably thought she was insane. She had never explained why she had freaked out in the gazebo, and now they had passed one another in the hallway of the lab, half shy, half professional recognition. Hugo dared to ask her once about Eliot:

"Are you—can I say—going out?" He looked mischievous as usual, but with an odd curiosity about his eyes and his tone of voice.

"*Non!*" She had responded with great haste and determination to squelch rumors. News traveled fast in the small world of their research group, and she didn't want anything coming back to Eliot. *Except if I could come back to him.* She shook herself. *How absurd. I was never with him.*

In this pool of both discovery and confusion, she would be glad to fly away for a while and be scarce. She fancied herself a migratory bird, direction home, shedding her downy winter coat in a trail of feathers behind her. That process had already begun. Despite the disapproving looks of most of her neighbors, she had been flaunting shirt sleeves for weeks in Paris. *Oh, loh, loh.* Well-meaning French grandmothers, clad in neutral hues from head to toe, had clucked their tongues looking her up and down, while shaking their gray, coiffed heads in disbelief. One of the bolder biddies taught her a French proverb, perhaps hoping that the singsong quality of the words would remind this *drôle d'oiseau, or* "silly bird," to do the right thing. *"En avril, ne te découvre pas d'un fil; en mai, fais ce qui te plaît."* Thinking through the rhyme, she had never been able to render it satisfactorily in English, but the meaning was clear: stay bundled up until May. Privately thinking this ridiculous, she politely countered with "March goes in like a lion and out like a lamb," which usually tickled the ladies' fancies. They had not yet reached the end of March, and the weather was already warmer than May in Claire's corner of Canada. Even now, Mom would probably have to meet her at the airport at home with her parka. Who else would meet her? Her heart sank as she thought of her older brother, and wondered where he really was.

***

The blue walls of the guestroom in her parents' house always had a chill in the winter, being on the north side of the house. Claire pulled on the handle of the stiff closet door, looking for an extra afghan to ward off the cold air. She caught a glimpse of a familiar burgundy crocheted edge above her head, and tugged it down, nearly bringing a cardboard box down on top of her head in the process.

In the dim light, she read the square cardboard box marked in the even-handed, Sharpie cursive of her mother: "paper, glue gun, stencils." A stash of forgotten crafts. The three items listed formed a pattern that gave Claire an idea of what else there might be inside, like points in an asterism, the grouping of stars that gave the observer an idea of the smaller images and meanings within. "Art supplies"—maybe there was a clutch of pens. She always needed pens. She flipped open the dusty brown flaps of the cardboard easily and peered inside.

Rather than the expected stacks of paint-gummed plastic and stiff brushes, her eyes fell upon an odd assortment of shapes and colors, a mini-landscape that recalled to mind an era, a relationship, a forgotten joy. The first item she drew out was Peter's star machine, about the size of a large round loaf of bread. The black dome on the top was pricked with hundreds of holes of various sizes—she ran her fingers over the surface, like a sort of reverse braille, remembering the patterns that would project on the smooth ceiling of Peter's bedroom when they darkened it with curtains and blankets stuffed around the edges. They couldn't get enough of the night sky at nighttime; they had to make it shine in the daytime, too. She flicked the switch on the bottom, the one that used to make the lamps of heaven lift and dazzle their eyes. Nothing. Maybe Mom had batteries downstairs.

Claire's things were mixed up in there, too. A turquoise cardboard pencil box embellished with

49

colorful motifs of superheroes in puffy stickers. Opening it, she drew in her breath sharply and tears unexpectedly stung her eyes from behind. It was her treasure and tool box from the "lab." Tables of measurements and clippings of cartoons were taped to the inside lid for quick reference. One by one, she drew out each item and considered its value. The mental furniture of her young life. How long had it been since she had seen these daily companions? A small, flat square box of cover slides. Several specimens permanently affixed to larger microscope slides, one label scrawled with "Algie." Loose wire strung with tiny vertebrae bones like some other little girl might have done with beads. Tiny jars from those hotel samples of jam Dad would bring home from time to time, emptied, filled with agates or bits of sea glass. A rusty scalpel, glass stirring rods that had miraculously remained unbroken through endless experiments.

Songs. She had also found a Joni Mitchell album in a slippery stack of loose CDs, mostly pirated and hand-marked by friends in high school. Joni's remorse-stricken voice moaned through her mind: "Just before our love got lost, you said I am as constant as a northern star; constantly in the darkness, where's that at?" The longing for a love that hung over her unfinished came back to her. The cowlick on the back of his head that stood up when he took his headphones off, his sideways smile that lined up when he looked up at her from his endless piles of equipment. She hardly knew him and yet she did. She suddenly realized that Eliot had never exacted anything from her. Except songs.

"Claire, baby!" Claire's mother's voice up the stairs broke through her drifting thoughts, and made the blood rush to her face.

"Yeah, mom?"

"It's time to eat! Did you find what you were looking for?"

"Yeah, I think so."

***

That evening, Claire had lingered as long as possible in the warm company of her parents, the half-yellow light of the dining room keeping their words just cozy enough—not too intimate. They spoke of Paris, not the past. She told them about Art, but not Eliot. She liked this in-between. It reminded her of weekends as a little girl, when she would climb into their bed clutching the Sunday morning paper, crawling over sprawled legs and arms to get in in the middle.

Now, she was stretched out on the bed alone in the blue room, cold toes tangled in a semi-warmth of an odd assortment of throw blankets. She rolled over, long legs restless for firm ground while her mind kept reaching back, refusing her a peaceful present. Reaching out, Claire flipped a small pool of lamplight onto the wooden floor, and turned to a page of fresh white paper. The emptiness and potential on the surface made her excited and apprehensive. She wrote in her journal, but carefully tore it out afterward. There was something about a letter, never mind if she never got around to sending it.

***

Dear Eliot,

I am back in Manitoba and all the birds that I told you about are down for the night. There used to be a nightingale that would coo around four in the morning, and it's nearly that time now. But for the moment, I think I am the only one awake. Except that you are, too. Seven hours away?

P.S. Which is the bird that goes cheeeeep, cheeeeep, whap-whap-whap?

***

Beep-beep, bee-dadabeep, bee-dadabeep. Claire awoke with a start, the alarm piercing into the in-between of sleep and awake, daydreams mingling with nightly revelations. *5 am? On vacation? What the – ?* And then she remembered. Claire and her dad had been plotting for several days to make a trek to Sunset Beach. She tucked her chin into her chest and peered over the foot of the bed, glimpsing her careful arrangements from the night before. Hiking boots, camera, rucksack, pocketknife, compass. The last two items were seemingly unnecessary, and yet utterly proper to the lingering traces of her adventuresome girlhood. She slipped into layers of fleece and wool, and tiptoed down the long hallway, carefully avoiding the wooden planks that squeaked. *Pete taught me that, for sneaking out.*

Dad was downstairs, filling the large green thermos with coffee. It was the same color as his old, familiar down vest that outlined his shoulders. He turned around to her with a grin:

"You used to prefer hot chocolate for Sunset Beach, but I figured you're all grown-up now and need caffeine like the rest of us, when it's this early." Claire was busy rubbing the sandy feeling out of her eyes.

"Yeah, I didn't sleep much. Still-" She paused, wondering how much to say. "Still getting over jetlag, I guess."

"Yup, I suppose. Now, how do you say it over there—Alone zee?" Claire tilted her head, pondering the unfamiliar syllables, until a smile grew into a gentle giggle.

"Yeah, Dad. *Allons-y.*"

***

It was still dark, but the moon was setting, its cool cast of silvery, shivering blue soon to be replaced by warm, spreading yellows and oranges. The frigid car bumped over the frozen back roads, unplowed but packed into uneven patches of sand and ice.

"We got a midwinter melt, oh, about two weeks back," Dad was explaining. Claire was listening with half an ear, her thought-filled gaze had already traveled far away over the familiar stretches of prairie grasses, reaching back in time to the days when she and Peter would make this same expedition with their father to Sunset Beach. Yes, there were days before sadness. Maybe they had fought over stupid things like Sunday comics, but they were still friends, equals. Not estranged. Claire stole a glance at her dad, trying to decide whether she should bring up her older brother. Half an hour previous in the kitchen, she had noticed for maybe the first time how white his hair was; not all of his wrinkles were the crinkly type, around the eyes. Still half-asleep, unedited questions flashed across her mind. *What would I ask Dad if I dared?*

***

Do you still see him as a little boy? He always laughed, rarely mocked. You remember his first steps, his first telescope, holding his little sister, propped up on the couch with a proud grin, the framed photo on the mantelpiece said so. Careful of her head, her neck isn't strong enough yet to support the weight. His hands pat her crocheted blanket, wrists still thick with his own baby fat, so soft. What happened to your son so strong? He got lost on the way home, the spiraling down of the bottle as it swirls into one more glass. Nights spent waiting for the startled hum of the garage door, indicating return. You used to go for walks, just to shake off the knots in your stomach at 2 a.m., I heard you leave. I just thought you liked to go for walks.

***

They stood on the gravelly shores, waiting for the first blush. Claire stood motionless as if the dawn were a skittish bird. It crept up very slowly at first.

"Dad?" The sky was starting to manifest its glory.

"Yeah, Clairebelle?" She paused, heart pounding in her ears in the silence of delayed response — *should I?*

"Where is Peter?" So raw, so much it hurt. It hurt him to hear that name, she knew it did, and yet she could not rest, could not let the day break without some kind of understanding, even a broken one. Her question ripped through miles and years all at once. He was looking right at her, taken aback.

55

"Well, Claire, you know as much as mom and I do."

"Really?" Her tone had a hint of doubt. *What if I know more than they do?*

"You don't think we'd keep something from you, do you?" Claire weighed this possibility, and realized that this was probably true. She herself had been the one to keep things hidden. As the coral sky burned in front of them, she imagined how nice to would be to cast some of her mental photographs into that flame. Crumpling in the blaze, faces hidden forever would sink into the water below. That would be freedom, baptism and fire. Scenes came rushing to the fore, and she finally let go, throwing them out into the open air.

"Dad, do you remember when I got grounded for taking money from Mom's purse? It was Pete. He said he'd make my life miserable at school if I didn't."

"Oh, Claire."

"He used to bully me . . . a lot."

"Well, *that's* wrong. I s'pose you guys roughhoused a bit."

"Those bruises . . ."

He turned and looked sharply at her, no longer at the sky.

"From Pete."

"He *hit* you?" Disbelief and quick sorrow, bitterly combined.

"Oh, Dad."

By the time she finished, the sun was high and bright, and the glare on the choppy waves stung her tear-exhausted eyes. Knees to her chest, Dad's hand on her back. Empty. But beginning to be free.

***

The remainder of Claire's holiday in Manitoba lent itself to a few more quiet conversations with her parents about her older brother over the years. The way that tears leaped to her mother's eyes indicated perhaps that this was the culmination of her worst fears, suspecting "all along" that something was amiss, yet somehow unable to pinpoint it. The benefit of the doubt, extended so long and with open-hearted trust, had been betrayed. Mom and Dad grieved with Claire when she needed them, and held one another up in the dim kitchen light for support and comfort when they thought she had gone to bed. Claire remembered that this was an old habit of theirs, standing, leaning, quietly saying their prayers together.

How many old deceits were there, woven together till one? They began to painfully disentangle one thread from another and a kind of story grew out of the mess. Peter had certainly mistreated Mary, his ex-wife. That seemed to speak for itself, with the letters Claire had discovered. Pete hadn't always been that way, but chose to let the dark in, bit by bit. A little selfishness, short in his replies, sullen. Grabbed her by the arm ("Peter! That hurts!") Then, the white nights, half-drunken calls, Dad's sad, gray walks in the moonlight. Claire could still see his bent head, silhouetted, coming up the driveway when she peeked outside her window. She wanted to go to him, to offer and take assurance that they were a family still. Maybe even that she'd have her big brother back someday. It was exhausting, coming to terms with it all. They had to go back, edit, and rewrite twenty-odd years of life.

With these disclosures came a new intimacy between them. Sometimes it felt like a betrayal, or a trampling of the good memories. She was turning her back on the hope that this had all been her imagination. In the end, Claire was relieved when her return date came around, and she followed her father out to the truck with her bags for the long drive to the airport. She had been lonesome for Paris, for the lady at the *boulangerie* and her perky idiosyncrasies — *ça va très bien, ma foi!* — and the smells of the city. She pulled out her journal to remember the place to which she was returning while the 747 jets underneath her rumbled and prepared for takeoff.

***

Asphalt warmed by the sun except when I step over the vents and a wave of dry heat blows over me that smells of métro. They must use the same solution to disinfect those tunnels — probably haven't changed the product in sixty years. Like a woman who discovers Chanel No. 5. Why ever change? This is not a city given to rash alterations. Will anything be different when I return? Countless people come in and out, move there and move away, and yet nothing seems to change. I know that when I walk down rue St. Paul, it will be as always, first the heady scent of pain au chocolat they keep in the little heater at the corner café, then diesel exhaust, then the rotisserie chickens outside the butcher shop, maybe the fleeting perfume of a passing Parisienne, the pungent cheese shop, and finally, fresh-cut flowers at that exotic fleuriste. The landscape remains the same. It is the people who are unpredictable.

***

Thankfully Art was predictable in the right sort of way. Eliot had been a solid, happy reality — for a time. Claire had gathered from the lab gossip that he was in England for his research. *Probably to see a girl.* She surprised herself with the immediate jealousy of someone she did not know and perhaps did not even exist.

One afternoon, after she had been back for a number of days, she was nearing the south corner of the *Jardin de Luxembourg*, striding the long way from St.

Michel to Port-Royal. She was thinking of Peter. The sun came flashing in and out through the clouds, feathers scooting across a pale blue canvas in dramatic grayish purple and white. Once Claire had laid in the prairie grass under such a sky back home, and the straight-line winds suddenly blasted all living things down flat, the sky turned green, and mom's faint shouting for her mingled with the sirens screaming all around, find shelter. They all cried for her. Here, it was just another windy Wednesday in Paris, the first of the month, and the routine alarms rang all around the city.

In his wanderings, they knew that Peter had been in Paris, too. Maybe that was the initial attraction for Claire. She cast her eyes to the tops of the odd, squared trees of the esplanade and down to the sandy playgrounds. Maybe he had walked here with his friends, lovers, colleagues. The *observatoire* was finally in view, that bulbous mass of white that looked like a large weather balloon about to pop. She mused over that picture — the planetarium exploding, sending stars flying and scattered over the dewy grass in the morning. Fantastical image. Peter once said something about the imagination of the ancients, how the patterns barely looked like the names they were given, and how science and imagination must work hand-in-hand. In truth, the dome of observation was highly inflexible, strong steel joists that housed the annals of rigid astronomic research. Knowing her love for the night sky, he once sent her a postcard with the Luxembourg Gardens in the background, "Love, Peter." It had given her hope. But that was the last piece of him she had left. In response, she had sent a postcard, touristic to the hilt, the glossy front decorated with grizzlies, wildflowers, lakes. *Welcome to Manitoba!* in garish pink across the front. She got it back a few weeks later, stamped with "retour à l'expéditeur."

She decided to lift her spirits with a *chocolat chaud* at the café on the corner. Despite the brisk wind, she preferred to be outdoors on the patio. Crouched over her cup, warm steam filling her vision, she sat and privately enjoyed her brooding and blurred view behind the fog on her glasses.

"Claire?" A surprised voice sent her name across the terrace. She looked up. It was Hugo, his curvy grin emerging from a floppy, sleek mop of black hair.

"Hugo!" She was actually happy to see him, a familiar person in a large city. "How are your holidays? Did you go home?"

"*Non*, I must stay in France for my visa right now. If I go to Columbia now, they won't let me back in." Claire stuck out her lower lip in sympathy, but Hugo quickly added: "Of course, my girlfriend's family in Aix—they were content to welcome me for Easter."

"Your *girlfriend*?" Claire tried not to sound incredulous, but it didn't work. Hugo guffawed.

"But yes, I *do have* one!" emphasizing the syllables in his particular way. He didn't seemed offended at Claire's reaction, only amused. "I guess you must have seen your boyfriend when you were home in Manitoba, *euh*?" Claire was startled. *Why did everyone seem to assume — ?*

"Why, *non*, I didn't in fact. I don't have a boyfriend."

"Ah, then my friend was wrong all along."

"Friend?"

"Oh, just a friend." He looked sly.

"Someone I know . . . as a friend?"

"It is possible, yes." He slipped out the chair across from her, looking across the park. "Anyway, I leave you now." Claire gave him a bewildered look. He excused himself with the customary kisses on her cheeks, now warm with excitement. "See you back in the lab soon." Claire nodded a confused goodbye, and shook her head as she dug the *euros* out of her pocket. She was late herself, to meet Art.

***

She climbed the familiar worn steps that spiraled up to Art's apartment. She wanted to get there, because it meant that she could relax. She paused on the landing

62

and tilted her head side-to-side, stretching her sore neck. When she reached the door, however, she discovered a note: "*Ran off to the cheese woman. On the boulevard, halfway down.*" Claire smiled, and chided her friend. *Running off to the cheese woman without my consent!* She turned and headed to the Sunday market.

The *marché* had been a recent discovery for Claire, and she loved every minute of it. Three times a week, a long line of permanent green tents stretched its way down the winding road behind Art's apartment, rain or shine. The feast of smells, sights, and sounds provided her with more nourishment than the food itself. As she elbowed her way through the mêlée of grocery carts, children and dogs, she caught the eye of the fruit seller that gave her a free melon two weeks ago—and smiled a shy *bonjour*. Then there was the butcher from whom she bought a few links of merguez sausage every week. Though her meager request seemed cheap and unfair to a French butcher who took pride in the finest cuts of beef, he never slighted her. Claire had watched the scale as he calculated, always rounding down, throwing a little extra in once it had been weighed. She would have to think of some way of thanking him—she nodded at him while she passed, mouthing the words *à bientôt*, hoping he wasn't offended. Now where was that cheese lady of Art's?

Finally, she reached the booth with pyramids of Camembert, fresh leaf-wrapped *chèvre*, and a young woman behind the case who was presently being completely charmed by Art's wiles. She signaled to Art, whose eyes lit up even more, as if the attention of two young ladies was really more than he could have hoped for.

"Claire! *Alors,* you must have found my note, then?"

"Yes, Art. *Merci.* You're looking well!"

"Euh? These old bones? Bah." Art cast an eye her direction while arranging his arms around a baguette, a carton of eggs, and a flat of clementines. Claire offered to take most of his parcels. He shook his head.

"Nay, *ma fille.*" He shot a glance to a nearby café table. "Let's get a coffee here and I can rest a spell."

Inserting themselves into the tableau that is a Parisian café, Claire hand-picked the most vivid and cheerful stories from her break in Manitoba. Carefully, she managed to sidestep the monumental sadness, hoping to save it for another time. Art brought the conversation around to returning to work.

"Oh yes!" Claire answered. "Funny thing, I bumped into my lab partner Hugo today."

"Indeed." His bushy eyebrows grew higher. "In*deed*." Even higher. She suddenly realized his meaning.

"Oh Art! I'm not interested in *Hugo*!" He looked genuinely surprised.

"Euh? Say what? Well-well-why were you mooning around with him in the garden?" Here, Claire couldn't help blushing as she found herself thinking about the convergence of moons, gardens, and another man entirely. "You sure seemed happy with him, chucklin' and what not." Claire tried to imagine when this could have been—a coffee break?

"Oh Art, we're just lab partners. Nothing more!" She smiled.

"Well, I guess there's no harm in that. Hee!" Art started wheezing with bursts of laughter at his own mistake. "But you know, Marie and Pierre Curie were workmates in that building over there." He pointed. "Until—"

"No way, not me, not Hugo. He's got a girlfriend anyway. *Huh, even silly Hugo had a girlfriend.*

"Then, I'd reckon you've still got a chance at your beau—the real one," Art offered.

"Thanks Art." She looked at him gratefully. "But how about that breakfast?"

***

The daily routine at the lab continued much in the same way as before, except that Claire was busier than ever, preparing her materials for the field research she would be doing in the Camargue in three weeks. The Institute had approved her for two months in the muggy salt marshes of the South of France, and she was looking forward to getting out of the city for a while. The monotony of the laboratory hallways, the dank smell of the lunchroom was beginning to chafe at her—especially since Eliot's bird-like whistle was nowhere to be found. Still in Cambridge. Maybe he had met someone else. She imagined what kind of willowy figure would have caught his eye. *Probably someone with gorgeous, abundant hair and a Fullbright. Maybe an Australian. Did Australians get Fullbrights?*

"Claire?" She jumped out of her thoughts—and her skin. Suddenly, there he was. A tall, thin apparition right in front of her, looking awkward and solemn all at once.

"What are you doing here?" Claire blurted out, her acute knowledge of his whereabouts betrayed in her surprised tone. For a fleeting instant, his eyeglasses twinkled half-amused, then immediately returned to a certain gravity.

"Ehm, I found something that belongs to you, I think." He held up a piece of paper, familiar folds betrayed the note she had received from her mother several weeks previous.

"Hey, where did you get that?" she asked angrily.

"Don't be annoyed. I put on a lab coat this morning, and it was in the pocket." He decided to venture further, throwing caution to the wind. "I don't get it."

"What?" she queried, snatching it from his hand. She looked around carefully to make sure they were alone, then cast her eyes over the words silently. It was the last bit of Peter she could recall, just her diary entry after the last time he called, only three years ago. The feeble, broken voice in her head croaked the pitiful, time-worn lines.

***

I can still hear his mocking-bird voice. His last phone message, I wore the tape thin listening and weeping. The belligerent monotone that hardly seemed like him. His voice, but dead (dying). Drunk, in any case. "Got married. Guess I'm in Spain for a while — ha! [crackle]. Dunno when we'll be back. Bye."

***

"Uh—" She stalled, with trembling lips. Hot anger began to raise her hackles.

"If he's married, why aren't you over him? It's none of my business, but I'm worried about you . . . please tell me, Claire." *So he had read it. How dare he?* She was poised to shoot back that it was none of his business, but instead found herself saying:

"Get over my own brother?" She ripped the words out of her. He tilted his head, puzzled. "It's my brother, okay? I don't want to talk about it anymore."

"Hang on a minute," he pleaded, "please don't move." With that, he unexpectedly vanished into the hallway, leaving her perched on her stool. She wondered where he had gone, but tried not to care. *It's always better not to care too much — it hurts less in the long run.* Suddenly, a crash from the other room startled her. She hopped off of her stool to find the cause of the commotion.

In the next room, Eliot was in the middle of a pile of cables and small black boxes. He heard her come in, whipped around and said,

"Well, some of these will do. Do you trust me?"

"Wha—" she began, but never finished. "Yes," she admitted in a hushed voice. *I really do.*

"Then take this mic." She quelled the rising irritation in her chest. *What is this? Another bid for free help?* She held out her hand, he passed it to her, and his other hand closed over hers. Claire's heart flip-flopped, and her mouth went dry.

"I think we need to go for another walk," he said calmly.

***

Soon they were heading south on the B line. The belligerent train cut a definitive track through the earth and under the Seine, from north to south. Some of the seats were empty, but they both remained standing in the rumbling car, the mood quiet and intense. Claire stared at their hands, a few inches apart. They gripped the center pole, shined to perfection by tens of thousands of slipping fingers. Eliot's nails faced her, square and white, bordered by a thin layer of gray, barely perceptible. Claire recalled one of her first biology lab assignments in the eighth grade: swab under fingernails; perform bacterial analysis on whatever you find. She wondered what Eliot's would betray, swiped on a fresh petri dish, the stories emerging overnight in varied colors and shapes. *I, too, could hunt you.* She backed up from the pole and her eyes refocused. *Uh — that's just a little too weird.*

His gaze was direct and steady, destination sure, while the train careened playfully through the underground tunnels. Dozens of questions swarmed in her head and died before they reached her tongue. There seemed to be a calm pact of silence that they were both meant to observe. The few other passengers eyed their odd bundles of black recording equipment warily. Eliot finally reached for the shiny knob, and the doors flew apart to the open air of *Cité Universitaire*. They mounted the steps to the front of the station, and past the bright blue iron bars of the *Parc Montsouris*.

"Do you think you can climb over that?" Eliot finally spoke halfway through the park, near a secluded corner of bushes and brush. He was pointing to the dark green plastic covering on a nearby fence.

"Why on earth —?" Her patience was stretched to the thinnest sheet of a mask.

"You said you trusted me." She had no answer to this. Casting a careful eye around, she stuck an edge of her scuffed shoes in the diamond-shaped wire and hoisted herself over. Hopefully there weren't any guards around. She quickly crouched and swung her other leg over.

"All right!" Eliot encouraged her. "Now, hang on —" His voice trailed away as she dropped herself to the ground. She found herself in a small, calm square, perhaps six feet by six feet. The air was green and cool, soothing her confused thoughts. Peace, and for the first time in months. She didn't mind waiting anymore. The canopies of two grand oaks reached straight up and over, intermingling into one great roof above. She leaned against one of the trees thoughtfully. *The woman and the tree. The man and the tree.*

"All right," Eliot, muffled, faraway. "Look down." A mic and headphones came wiggling through the wood chips and dirt at her feet, and she grabbed them, putting the headphones on as she had done on their previous outings.

"Okay, now what am I supposed to do with it?"

"Sing." Was the unexpected reply, clear through the headphones.

"Huh?"

"Sing."

"I don't sing."

"Then tell me about your brother." She felt lightheaded, then real anger. Deep, uncovered, unhealed, unfelt until this moment. Bursting out in the open like the scolding of an angry blackbird, she chipped and chirped staccato syllables.

"What the hell?" There goes the peace.

"What does he do?" She squatted down closer to the silver mesh of the microphone laying in the wood chips, trying to glare at him underneath the fence.

"Last time I checked, he was an astronomer."

"What *did* he do?" She cocked her head.

"He left us."

"Why?"

"He shook me. He whipped me around so hard, I couldn't turn my head for days. I told mom I got a crick in my neck from sleeping in an odd position." Silence on the other end. It lasted so long that Claire began to wonder whether she had scared him away. "He slapped me across the face, and I never told anyone either. I'm no

71

tattletale." She corrected herself, "I *wasn't*." For the first time since she could remember, she was letting her feelings take a direct voyage, non-stop, to spoken words. She forgot where she was, tears streaming down her cheeks, behind the blind, singing out her sad refrain. "What if he finds out I told someone?" Even as she expressed this familiar fear, she realized she was finally safe. *Peace.* Thrusting her head up to the branches reaching up, her mind flashed back to Rousseau's words: "the heavenly bodies are set far away from us . . . very long ladders are needed to get to them and bring them within our reach." A tiny despair deep inside of her expanded like a little bubble—no one can reach me here. Can they?

The other voice, the beautiful one, came swooping into her ears again, sweet the words:

"Can I come in now?"

"Yes, Eliot." She heard the chain link metal behind her jangle, followed by a thump on the ground. She turned and smiled through her tears at the tall, fair boy across from her.

"Can you sing with me here, too?" He reached tenderly around and lifted her hair, rubbing the nape of her neck. It was a gesture commonplace rather to longtime lovers, when their histories reached back.

"Claire, Claire. I want to help you." His hand slipped into hers, and they both slid to the ground, their

72

backs each held by a strong oak. This way, face-to-face, they talked until dusk drew near. The young couple hardly heard the shrill whistles of the guardsmen informing visitors to leave the park, their own melodies more compelling and true. Finally, after the winding tales came down to a trickle, Eliot checked the time on the glowing blue square of his cell phone. Home now. He walked her to her street, and they parted ways with three kisses.

***

On my back, the stars above. Familiar lines crisscross and weave a story both old and new. The Hunter looms larger, detaching from map and order, his pinpoints arcing down. Breathless. I let him touch my face, brush my cheeks with sparks. First the right, then the left. I wait for him to speak, but instead he turns quickly to the North, his arms windmilling into position with bow and arrow. A streak flies from his chest into a flock of waiting birds, stars exploding. He haunts me, hunts me, and finally sets me free.

ABOUT THE AUTHOR

Abbey von Gohren is currently on faculty at Trinity School at River Ridge in Eagan, MN. Prior to this, she taught French as a graduate instructor at the University of Minnesota Twin Cities and English and Creative Writing at the University of Paris VII, Charles V.

She spends most of her days teaching her students at how to wrap their lips and throats around the delicate sounds of the French language, remember Latin noun declension endings, and savor the wistful, salt-saturated voyage in the *Odyssey* or the dark beauty of Sophocles. She relishes daily, fascinating conversations with her fellow teachers about the intersections of literature, science, history, and a myriad other disciplines.

She devotes nearly every other stolen moment (including summer vacations) deciding what next to put on paper herself. She actively writes short essays on her blog, www.lifelongfling.blogspot.com, which began as a record of travels and developed into a forum for varied musings on life, beauty, God, and the world.

Fledgling Song (2013) is Abbey's first published fictional work.

Abbey lives in Minneapolis in a 1953 rambler with her husband, Karl. They are filling the space in their new home with books, vinyl records, and musical instruments at an alarming pace.

Made in the USA
Charleston, SC
14 March 2014